Wilson, Do You See It?

By Diane Van Wart

Illustrations by Monika Hansen

PEANUT
BUTTER
PRESS

Peanut Butter Press
9-1060 Dakota Street
Winnipeg, MB R2N 1P2
www.peanutbutterpress.ca

The artwork in this book was rendered in watercolour.
The text is set in Stone Serif.

Book design by Melanie Matheson, Blue Claw Studio.
Printed and bound in Hong Kong by Paramount Printing Company Limited / Book Art Inc., Ontario, Canada.

This book is Smyth sewn casebound.

10 9 8 7 6 5 4 3 2 1

LIBRARY AND ARCHIVES CANADA CATALOGUING IN PUBLICATION

Van Wart, Diane, 1953-, author
          Wilson, do you see it? / written by Diane Van Wart
; illustrated by Monika Hansen.

ISBN 978-1-927735-03-9 (bound)

          1. Animals--Manitoba--Identification--Juvenile fiction.
I. Hansen, Monika, 1956-, illustrator   II. Title.

√PS8643.A684W55 2013   jC813'.6   C2013-906830-9

M. Hansen

Dedicated to Luella Nichol

Author Diane Van Wart was a neighbour of Monika Hansen, the illustrator. Together they loved nature as they saw it in their own backyards in East Selkirk, Manitoba. This was the inspiration for the book.

This book is dedicated to their dear friend, Luella Nichol. Luella, also a neighbour of theirs, loved sitting in her kitchen looking out at the wildlife in her backyard. She especially loved feeding the birds and watching the deer. We miss you, Luella.

Little Hare is curious.

He wants to learn about the world around him.

He knows he can get help from his friend Wilson.

"Wilson, do you see it?"

"See what, Little Hare?"

"Over there in the woods.

It has four long legs, brown fur and

a black nose."

"Oh, that's…

a deer, Little Hare."

Little Hare glances up.

"Wilson, do you see it?"

"See what, Little Hare?"

"Over there up high in that tree.

It's brown with big claws

and a sharp beak."

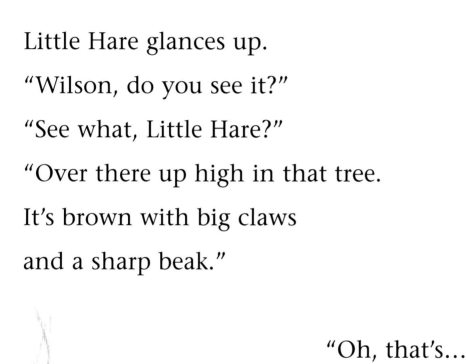

"Oh, that's...

an owl, Little Hare."

From the corner of his eye,

Little Hare sees something move.

"Wilson, do you see it?"

"See what, Little Hare?"

"Over there on that branch.

It's smaller than me and has

four legs, reddish fur

and a fluffy tail."

"Oh, that's...

a squirrel, Little Hare."

Just then Little Hare

notices another animal.

"Wilson, do you see it?"

"See what, Little Hare?"

"Over there down low in the bushes.

It's tiny and has two wings,

grey feathers on its back and a

black head."

"Oh, that's…

a chickadee,

Little Hare."

"Wow, Wilson! We've seen so many animals."

As Wilson walks on, he says...

"Yes, Little Hare, but let's keep looking."

Little Hare sees something
moving up and down.
"Wilson, do you see it?"
"See what, Little Hare?"
"Over there at the feeder.
It's blue with a white tummy
and a tuft of feathers on its head."

"Oh, that's...

a blue jay, Little Hare."

Little Hare spies something
scurrying on the ground.
"Wilson, do you see it?"
"See what, Little Hare?"
"Over there under the feeder.
It's much smaller than me with whiskers,
round ears and a thin tail."

"Oh, that's…

a mouse, Little Hare."

Little Hare watches
an animal trotting along.
"Wilson, do you see it?"
"See what, Little Hare?"
"Over there by the fence posts.
It's bigger than me
with reddish fur, a pointy nose
and a bushy tail."

                           "Oh, that's...

a fox, Little Hare."

Little Hare observes something
standing close by.

"Wilson, do you see it?"

"See what, Little Hare?"

"Over there near your red doghouse.

It's much bigger than me with a pink head,
blue body and four yellow paws."

"Oh, that's...

a child, Little Hare."

"HEY, WILSON!

Are you coming?

There's so much more to see!"